THE BROKER'S GAMBIT

JT BALDWIN

"The art of information brokerage isn't knowing everything—it's knowing what questions to ask, and more importantly, what questions not to ask. The moment you start thinking you understand the whole game is the moment you realize you've been playing checkers while everyone else moved to chess."

— Rhowan Cade, reflecting on his education in continental politics

Series Guide | THE PALISADE JOURNALS

RECOMMENDED READING ORDER:

CHRONOLOGICAL TIMELINE:

PART ONE

CANTON CUSK

Late Winter, 2189

North York, Continental Authority (CA)

— ❖ —

Information was currency to Rhowan Cade, and the invoice in front of him might as well have been minted gold—if only he could figure out why.

He held it up to the weak winter light filtering through frost-covered windows, checking the paper stock and watermarks. The weight felt right, the letterhead embossing caught the light properly, and when he brought it close to his nose, it carried the faint chemical scent of legitimate government printing.

Whatever this was, it wasn't fake. Which made it infinitely more interesting.

This morning, hunched over his desk in the drafty warehouse office with frost clinging to the windows like silver accusations, he was staring at an invoice that made absolutely no sense.

Canton Cusk processing waste - 47 barrels - Premium grade - Destination: Two Harbors Industrial - Payment: 340 crowns

Three hundred and forty crowns for Canton Cusk waste. Nearly five months' wages for a dock worker, paid for a single shipment of fish refuse. Canton Cusk were bottom-dwelling creatures so ugly and inedible that most boats threw them back rather than waste dock space. Their processing waste was typically dumped back into the harbor.

Nobody paid four months' salary for garbage. Not unless it wasn't garbage.

Rhowan set down the invoice and reached for the battered radio unit mounted beside his desk. The metal casing was cold enough to sting his fingertips, and when he pressed the transmission button, his breath clouded in the frigid air.

"Tara, you got a minute? I have a question about an invoice."

Static hissed through the speaker, mixing with distant sounds of forklift engines and cargo chains rattling beyond his cubicle walls. The radio's amber display flickered weakly in the gray morning light.

"What is it now, Cade? Can't it wait?" Tara's voice crackled back, distorted by interference and barely audible over heavy machinery grinding in the background.

"Canton Cusk processing waste shipment to Two Harbors Industrial. Payment shows three hundred and forty crowns. Does that strike you as—"

"Canton Cusk? What...?" Tara's voice cut through the static, suddenly sharper. The transmission broke off mid-word, leaving only the radio's electronic hum and the rhythmic clank of a loading crane somewhere in the warehouse depths. "Hang on."

The radio clicked off with a hollow snap that echoed in his small cubicle. Rhowan could hear boots on concrete getting louder—someone walking with purpose across the warehouse floor, their footsteps punctuated by the wheeze and hiss of hydraulic equipment and distant shouts of dock workers coordinating a cargo lift.

Two minutes later, Tara Verelli appeared in his doorway, wiping fish grease from her hands with a rag that had seen better decades. Her expression carried irritation reserved for people who'd been pulled away from actual work to deal with paperwork questions.

"You couldn't figure this out yourself?" she asked, not bothering to hide her annoyance. Oil stains darkened her work gloves, and the smell of diesel fuel and hydraulic fluid clung to her coveralls. "I've got three cargo containers that won't fit through the loading bay and a forklift that's making sounds like a dying cat. Probably needs a new propane tank switched out. Great idea to store the new tanks three buildings over."

As if summoned by her words, a grinding mechanical screech echoed from the warehouse floor, followed by someone cursing loudly enough to be heard over the general din of cargo operations.

"Just wanted to verify the pricing," Rhowan said, offering his most disarming smile—the one that usually worked on territorial administrators and customs officials. "Three hundred forty crowns for fish waste seems... ambitious."

Tara glanced at the invoice. But Rhowan caught the slight hesitation, the way her eyes lingered on the destination line.

"Payment clears, shipment moves, not my problem. Check the historical files if you're worried about pricing discrepancies." She turned to leave, movements just a bit too sharp. "Main office keeps the records."

"But does it seem—"

"Cade." She fixed him with a look that could have frozen the harbor. "I don't have time to verify every invoice that crosses your desk. My job is moving cargo, not explaining why someone's stupid enough to overpay for fish slop."

After she departed—her heavy boots echoing down the concrete corridor as she muttered something about clerks who couldn't handle basic paperwork—Rhowan sat back in his creaking desk chair. Dismissed but not satisfied. The faint smell of machine oil and her exasperation lingered in the small cubicle.

Too defensive. And that hesitation when she read the destination...

Tara Verelli had processed thousands of unusual shipments over the years. She'd seen everything from exotic livestock to questionable medical supplies pass through these docks. If Canton Cusk waste made her nervous, there was definitely more to this story.

He glanced around the warehouse office. Supervisor Henrik was conducting his morning inventory rounds, clipboard in hand, focused on legitimate concerns about legitimate cargo. The other clerks were absorbed in their own paperwork, processing the mundane business of territorial commerce.

Perfect.

He made his way to the filing room, where four seasons of shipping records were stored in wooden cabinets that smelled of salt air and bureaucratic neglect. The late winter wind rattled the windows as he pulled the files for the past year, spreading manifests across the dusty table that served for research nobody was supposed to be conducting.

The pattern was even more obvious when viewed across time. Every month, like clockwork: forty-seven barrels of Canton Cusk processing waste delivered to Two Harbors Industrial for the same premium price. Same tonnage, same destination, same payment schedule.

Forty-seven. Not fifty, not forty-five. Forty-seven. Too specific for rough estimation.

No legitimate industrial process required that kind of consistency for waste products. This was either the most peculiar business arrangement Rhowan had ever encountered, or someone was moving materials under a cover story that wouldn't attract attention from casual observers.

Rhowan leaned back in the dusty wooden chair, his mind racing through possibilities. What if this wasn't waste at all, but some kind of refined product? What if Canton Cusk contained something valuable that only a few people knew about? A secret that could make him very wealthy—or very dead, depending on who—

"Finding everything you need, Cade?"

Rhowan's chair scraped against the floor as he jolted upright, papers rustling in his sudden movement. Henrik stood in the doorway, his weathered face showing mild interest that could mean help or trouble.

"Checking discrepancies in the Canton Cusk invoices," Rhowan said, adopting the tone of someone performing due diligence rather than satisfying personal curiosity. "The pricing seems unusual for waste products."

Henrik stepped into the filing room and glanced at the spread manifests. His expression remained neutral, but Rhowan caught the way his eyes tracked the payment columns.

"Canton Cusk? Yeah, that's been going on for months. Strange business, but the payments clear and the shipments move on schedule." He shrugged, but it seemed forced. "Not our problem if someone wants to overpay for fish slop."

"Any idea what they're using it for?"

"Industrial processing, according to the manifest codes. Could be anything from fertilizer to chemical extraction." Henrik moved toward the door, clearly ending the conversation. "Two Harbors has processing plants for all kinds of specialized applications. Maybe they found a use for something everyone else throws away."

After Henrik departed, Rhowan remained at the table, studying the manifests with renewed focus. Two conversations, two people who both used the exact same phrase: "overpay for fish slop." Different words might be coincidence, but identical phrasing suggested coordination.

Someone's been coaching the staff.

He expanded his search to related materials, but paperwork only told part of the story. And his curiosity was beginning to gnaw at him like hunger—an intellectual itch that had made him excellent at information brokerage and occasionally terrible at personal safety.

He swiveled his chair toward the warehouse opening, watching dock workers guide cargo nets while cranes groaned overhead. Beyond the organized chaos of the harbor, gray water stretched to the horizon where fishing boats worked their nets against the winter sky.

The Northern Grace was out there somewhere, her blue hull cutting through the choppy water as she hauled in another catch of those grotesque bottom-dwellers. Captain Hendrick had no idea he was sitting on a mystery worth three hundred and forty crowns per shipment.

Rhowan stood and reached for the binoculars hanging on a peg near the window. He focused the lenses, scanning the distant boats until he found what he was looking for.

There she was. Working her nets methodically, probably cursing the weather and counting the hours until she could return to port with another load of Canton Cusk.

He lowered the binoculars, a slow smile spreading across his face. The smile that usually preceded either brilliant insights or catastrophically poor decisions.

"I know a guy," he murmured to himself.

Captain Hendrick owed him a favor from a cargo manifest mix-up Rhowan had quietly resolved last month. Small administrative errors could cost a fishing captain his license if the wrong official noticed. Information brokerage was all about maintaining relationships, and sometimes the best information came from people who did the actual work rather than those who just shuffled the paperwork.

By the time the lunch bell rang, he'd made a decision that would prove to be either brilliantly insightful or catastrophically stupid.

Knowing his luck, probably both.

Either way, Rhowan was confident he was on the cusp of something big. A discovery that separated professional information brokers from amateur clerks.

One that might finally get him noticed by people who operated beyond territorial politics.

✦

The afternoon was brutally cold, the cutting wind turning the harbor into an assault on exposed skin. Ice formed along the dock pilings, and the fishing boats that hadn't yet departed for their evening runs bobbed in water that looked black and hostile under the gray winter sky.

Rhowan made his way to the small boat rental that served the harbor's various needs—transportation to anchored vessels, emergency repairs, the occasional customs inspection that required mobility beyond the fixed docks. The proprietor, a grizzled man named Torven, looked skeptical about anyone wanting boat transport in this weather.

"You sure about this?" Torven called, eyeing the choppy harbor waters with professional concern. "It's nasty cold out there, and getting nastier. Wind's picking up from the northeast—that usually means ice by nightfall."

"Not really, but boss man has questions, and I need this job," Rhowan lied smoothly, showing his warehouse credentials with just enough confidence to suggest authority. "Need to verify cargo manifests with Captain Hendrick on the Northern Grace."

Boss man. Let Torven assume whatever level of importance seemed appropriate. People's imaginations usually created more impressive authority figures than reality provided.

Torven pocketed two steel chits and gestured toward a small skiff that looked barely adequate for the harbor conditions. "She'll get you there and back, but dress warm and hold tight. Water's mean today, and it's only getting meaner."

Twenty minutes later, Rhowan was questioning every decision that had led to this moment. The skiff bucked and pitched in the harbor chop, icy spray from the bow soaking through his heavy coat despite his attempts to stay clear of the worst of it. His hands were numb even inside thick gloves, and the salt spray had formed ice crystals on his beard.

This better be worth it, he thought, gripping the wheel as another wave sent freezing water cascading over the bow. Because dying of hypothermia for fish waste would be the most embarrassing epitaph in the history of information brokerage.

When he finally spotted the Northern Grace working her nets in the distance, he reached for the skiff's marine radio—a battered unit mounted near the wheel that looked like it had survived more storms than it should have.

He keyed the transmitter, static crackling through the speaker. "Northern Grace, Northern Grace, this is..." He realized he had no call sign. "This is the warehouse skiff requesting permission to come alongside."

Nothing but static and interference. The radio box had probably taken on water during the crossing. Rhowan gave it a firm thump with his fist— the universal repair technique for equipment that predated him—and the signal cleared enough to hear a voice through the electronic snow.

"...copy that, warehouse... come on then! Make it... loading dock side!"

The transmission dissolved back into static, but Rhowan had heard enough. He maneuvered the skiff against the fishing boat's hull, grateful when strong hands helped haul him aboard. Captain Hendrick was weathered and practical, moving with decades of efficiency earned on dangerous waters.

"Something important brought you out here," Hendrick said, leading him into the gloriously warm galley and handing him a steaming cup. The captain's eyes showed concern—he'd seen too many people underestimate winter waters. "Apologies, the good stuff doesn't last long out here. All we have is the cheap stuff at the moment. What brings you out in this mess?"

The coffee tasted like battery acid mixed with machine oil, but it was hot. Rhowan warmed his hands on the cup and pulled out the invoice, grateful to be somewhere the paper wouldn't blow away or get soaked.

"This vessel ID yours?"

Hendrick reached for the readers hanging around his neck and studied the paperwork carefully—official documents could make or break a fishing operation.

"Looks like it. Something wrong with the paperwork?"

"Not in the manner you might think." Rhowan paused, choosing his next words carefully. "What exactly is Canton Cusk?"

Hendrick's weathered face broke into a grin—the first genuine expression of pleasure Rhowan had seen from anyone when discussing those creatures.

"Ugliest damn fish in these waters. Bottom-dwellers, nasty to look at, worse to clean. Teeth like broken glass, skin that feels like wet sandpaper, and they smell like something died in a sewer." He gestured toward the deck where nets full of the grotesque creatures lay waiting. "Most boats won't even bother hauling them up—too much work for something nobody wants to eat."

"But you do."

"Different story entirely," Hendrick said, his grin widening. "Like clockwork—we pull enough into the boat, get a good month's pay, and move on to other catches we only wish paid as well. That money's been a blessing for this boat and crew. We got enough stowed away to run another four or five seasons without losing cash flow."

The captain's expression shifted to concern. "You ain't thinking this is a mistake, are you? Because I got to tell you, that money's been keeping families fed through the worst winter we've seen in years."

"No, no. I'm just thankful this good fortune landed on your boat," Rhowan said quickly, meaning it. Whatever was happening here, it was clearly benefiting people who deserved better than scraping by on irregular catches. "I was hoping to find more such work for you, if possible. Do you happen to know what happens after the catch hits the docks?"

"Processing," Hendrick said, moving to pour himself coffee from a pot that had probably been brewing since dawn. "The catch gets sent west to the northern docks—the ones they completed a couple years ago. There it gets processed and packaged into fifty-five gallon drums, then sent either by truck or rail to heaven knows where."

He shook his head in amazement. "Never in my life have I seen such fortune catching junk fish. My grandfather worked these waters, my father worked them, and now me. Three generations of Hendricks, and none of us ever made a living off bottom-feeders until now."

"Any idea why Canton Cusk specifically?"

"Can't say. But someone clearly knows something we don't." Hendrick's eyes showed wariness—he'd learned not to question good fortune too closely. "Far as I'm concerned, as long as the payments keep coming and nobody gets hurt, I'm happy to keep hauling the ugly bastards up."

Rhowan thanked the captain and prepared for the miserable journey back to shore, his eyes following the coastline west toward the new processing docks that gleamed in the winter light like monuments to industrial efficiency.

Processing into drums. Shipping to unknown destinations. Premium payments for waste products.

The pieces were starting to form a pattern, but it was still incomplete. Like studying a map with half the territory missing.

Back at the warehouse, he found Clara reviewing shipping schedules at her desk, her usual efficiency slightly hampered by having to wear gloves indoors due to the building's inadequate heating.

"The new warehouses west of here—Two Harbors Industrial, I think. You know much about them?"

Clara glanced up from her paperwork, breath visible in the cold air. "No direct connections to us. They moved in a little over a year ago. We thought they were going to start taking business from us, but they focus on other things. More specialized."

"Specialized how?"

"Chemical processing, from what I hear. Industrial applications for materials most people consider waste." She pulled her gloves tighter, clearly wanting to return to work before her fingers went numb. "They pay well for the right materials, but they're very particular about specifications."

Twenty minutes later, Rhowan was riding the coastal tram west, watching the industrial landscape roll past until he reached the newer section of the port. The tram was nearly empty—most workers had finished their shifts and gone home to warm fires and hot meals.

Two Harbors Industrial sat behind a chain-link fence, its buildings dark in the late afternoon light. The architecture was functional rather than aesthetic, designed for efficiency rather than appearance. But there was something about the layout that suggested more security than typical industrial processing required.

The main gate was locked, secured with chains and official-looking warnings about authorized personnel only. But a loading dock door on the building's north side hung slightly ajar—not enough to suggest invitation, but enough to suggest carelessness.

Rhowan paused at the fence line, weighing options. Trespassing on industrial property was significantly more serious than his usual information gathering activities—territorial charges rather than simple embarrassment.

But that slightly open door was practically beckoning to him.

Sometimes, he thought, the best information requires the worst decisions.

He found a section of fence where the chain-link had pulled away from its post, creating a gap just wide enough for someone of his build to squeeze through. A gap that definitely hadn't been there by accident, but which provided plausible deniability for anyone who might need it later.

Ignoring the voice in his head that warned against trespassing—the same voice that had prevented him from discovering several highly profitable information opportunities in the past—Rhowan slipped inside.

The smell hit him immediately: the awful reek of rotted fish mixed with chemical processing. But underneath that was something else—a metallic tang that reminded him of blood, and a sharp chemical odor that made his eyes water.

Rows of fifty-five gallon drums lined the warehouse walls, each marked with codes that meant nothing to him but suggested systematic organization. Shipping labels were stacked on a nearby table in neat piles, ready for application to outgoing cargo.

He grabbed one, squinting at the address in the dim light filtering through dirty windows:

Millhaven Maritime Solutions
1247 Industrial Harbor Way
Beltmoire

A concrete lead that might explain what all these "worthless" materials were actually being used for.

But as he pocketed the shipping label, he heard the distinctive sound of boots on concrete approaching the building. Multiple sets, moving with the purposeful coordination of security personnel.

Time to go.

He made his way back to the gap in the fence, moving as quietly as possible while fighting the urge to run. Running attracted attention, and attention was the last thing he needed right now.

The voices were closer now, discussing shift changes and inspection schedules. This facility operated under considerably more security than its industrial appearance implied.

Rhowan reached the fence line just as lights began coming on inside the building, revealing the true scale of the operation within. This wasn't just chemical processing—this was systematic production of something that required both secrecy and security.

What the hell have I stumbled into?

☼

The next morning, Rhowan approached Henrik with a request that felt simultaneously routine and life-changing.

"Personal leave," he explained, showing the properly completed forms that every territorial worker kept on file for family emergencies. "Need a few days to handle some family matters in Beltmoire."

Henrik approved the leave without question, probably assuming Rhowan needed to deal with winter-related problems that plagued everyone in the northern territories during the coldest months. Frozen pipes, heating failures, domestic crises that required immediate attention and territorial travel.

If only it were that simple.

Two hours later, Rhowan was aboard the eastbound Continental Express, watching the frozen landscape roll past the train windows as he traveled toward Beltmoire and what he hoped would be answers to questions that had been keeping him awake at night.

The train was comfortable enough, with basic amenities that made territorial travel bearable without being luxurious. Other passengers seemed to be conducting ordinary business—merchants, administrators, the occasional family traveling for perfectly legitimate reasons.

Unlike him, who was chasing shipping invoices and trespassing discoveries toward what might be the biggest information opportunity of his career.

Or the last mistake I ever make.

But when he finally found 1247 Industrial Harbor Way, his heart sank like a stone dropped in deep water.

It was a small machine shop specializing in marine engine repair, with a weathered sign advertising services for fishing vessels and cargo ships. Honest, practical business that kept the territorial economy functioning without attracting attention from continental authorities.

Nothing about it suggested the headquarters for a maritime solutions company that processed mysterious materials from across the northern territories.

"Never heard of them," the shop owner confirmed when Rhowan inquired about Millhaven Maritime Solutions. The man was a competent mechanic with grease under his fingernails and straightforward manner.

"Been here fifteen years, and this has always been Carlson's Marine Repair. Maybe they used to be here? Or maybe it's a mail drop service?"

Mail drop service. That would make sense for an operation that needed legitimate addresses without maintaining actual facilities.

By evening, his contact at territorial records—a clerk named Morrison who'd proven useful for previous information gathering activities—had confirmed his suspicions: Millhaven Maritime Solutions was a shell company, registered with the minimal paperwork required for legal existence but with no actual business operations.

Just another layer in what was becoming an increasingly complex puzzle.

Shell companies. False addresses. Premium payments for waste products. Chemical processing under security protocols.

As evening approached, Rhowan found lodging at a small inn that served the practical needs of territorial travelers—clean beds, hot meals, and discretion that asked no questions about why someone might need accommodation without advance notice.

He settled into a room that was comfortable without being memorable, designed to house people temporarily without encouraging them to linger. The inn's other guests seemed to be conducting legitimate business, their conversations focused on trade schedules and family obligations rather than mysterious shipping arrangements.

He was still puzzling over the freight codes and shell company connections when someone knocked on his door—not the casual rap of hotel staff, but the deliberate pattern of someone who wanted to be heard clearly.

Confident. Purposeful. Potentially dangerous.

Rhowan checked his appearance in the mirror—professional but not threatening, curious but not guilty—and opened the door to find a young woman who immediately redefined his understanding of dangerous.

She was perhaps thirty-three, wearing practical clothes that had seen hard use, and she carried herself comfortably in places where comfort usually required violence. Her left eye was a clouded, milky mess that spoke of deliberate damage—injury that sent messages rather than resulting from accidents.

But it was her right eye that captured his attention: sharp green-hazel, studying him with predatory intensity that suggested she was cataloging weaknesses while calculating their potential usefulness.

"Rhowan Cade?" she asked, her voice carrying the rough edges of someone who'd grown up on streets where politeness was a luxury most people couldn't afford.

Here we go.

"That depends," Rhowan said, offering his practiced smile while trying not to stare at her damaged eye. He found himself looking away, then back, uncertain whether his attention was making her uncomfortable or if she was beyond caring about such considerations. "Are you here with good news or bad news? Because I have to say, the evening's been disappointing enough already."

"You been sniffing around where you don't belong," she said, stepping into the room without invitation—casual violation of personal space that suggested either supreme confidence or complete indifference to social conventions.

"Well now, I'm sure there's been some misunderstanding," Rhowan said, his charm shifting into gear while he subtly positioned himself between her and his research materials. "I'm just a simple warehouse clerk conducting some routine business verification. Nothing that should concern anyone with such..." He gestured vaguely, trying to find words that acknowledged her obvious competence without sounding condescending.

"Cut the smooth talk," she interrupted flatly. "Simple warehouse clerk? Then what's a simple warehouse clerk doing all the way out here in Beltmoire?" Her good eye fixed on him with predatory focus that made him feel like prey being evaluated for processing. "Do you know who owns this city? I bet if your nosy brain knew that, you probably wouldn't have come here. But something did, and that earned you the wrong attention."

Rhowan's smile faltered as he realized his usual approach wasn't having its customary effect. This wasn't someone impressed by wit and good looks—this was someone who evaluated people based on entirely different criteria.

"I'm afraid I don't follow."

"Course you don't. You think you're clever, following paper trails and knocking on doors? You left tracks everywhere you went." She pulled a piece of paper from her coat with movements that suggested weapons might follow if the conversation went poorly. "Leave request at your job. Questions about fake companies. Your real name on the inn register. Machine shop owner ratted you out the moment he saw that baby face of yours asking about things nobody should know."

She wasn't just threatening him—she was demonstrating capabilities. Systematic intelligence gathering that suggested organization rather than freelance intimidation.

The charm offensive definitely wasn't working. Rhowan studied her more carefully, noting the way she positioned herself to control both his movements and her own escape routes. This wasn't someone who made amateur mistakes.

"And who exactly are you reporting to?" he asked, his tone becoming more serious as he recognized that this conversation would require different skills than he usually deployed.

"People who notice when someone starts connecting dots about Canton Cusk and Ferrosalt." She folded the paper with precise movements. "People who got questions about why you're so interested in their business."

"Ferrosalt?"

The word hit him like a physical blow. He'd heard whispers about Ferrosalt in conversations that happened between information brokers after too much alcohol and too little discretion. Strategic materials. Continental-level importance. Substances that appeared in rumors about experimental programs and disappeared people.

If Canton Cusk waste was connected to Ferrosalt acquisition, he'd stumbled into something considerably more dangerous than unusual shipping arrangements.

"You stirred up the wrong people, warehouse boy. Made them curious about what you think you know." She moved toward the door, clearly ending the conversation on her terms. "Boss wants to see you."

"Now, I'm confident we can work something out," Rhowan said, making one final attempt to find his footing in a conversation that had gone completely off the rails. "Whatever concerns your boss might have, I'm sure we can address them like civilized people."

She stopped and looked at him with something approaching pity—expression usually reserved for people who fundamentally misunderstood the nature of their situation.

"You really don't get it, do you? This isn't about being civilized. You stuck your nose in something big, and now you got two choices."

"Which are?"

"Come with me and maybe get some answers. Or don't come with me and maybe wake up floating in that harbor." She pointed toward the window, where evening light reflected off water that looked considerably less welcoming than it had that morning. "Boss prefers the first option, but she ain't married to it."

Rhowan felt his last vestige of confidence drain away like water through broken pipes. Whatever game he'd thought he was playing, the rules had just changed completely.

"Who is your boss?"

"Someone who knows what Canton Cusk waste actually gets used for. Someone who might be willing to explain it to you, if you're smart enough to shut up and listen." She opened the door with movements that suggested this conversation was over regardless of his preferences. "So, pretty nosy boy, grab your shit. People waitin'."

"Where are we going?"

"To meet people who can answer the questions that got you into this mess." Her expression remained flat, professional, giving away nothing about what those answers might cost him. "And to find out if you're worth keeping alive."

After she departed—leaving behind the scent of winter air and implied violence—Rhowan sat in his small inn room, staring at his research materials while the implications of the evening settled over him like a weight he definitely couldn't carry alone.

At twenty-two, he'd thought he was conducting sophisticated investigation into unusual shipping patterns. Instead, he'd been stumbling through a trail of amateur mistakes that had attracted attention from people who monitored territorial policy and operated through networks he hadn't known existed.

His investigation into Canton Cusk waste had evolved into something that involved shell companies, false addresses, and systematic material acquisition that mattered to people who made decisions about continental affairs.

Ferrosalt. Strategic materials. Disappeared people.

Tomorrow, he would discover what it meant to trade information at a level where amateur curiosity could either lead to education or simply disappear entirely.

He only hoped he was clever enough to survive the lesson.

And somewhere in the back of his mind, a small voice wondered if this was how real information brokers separated themselves from warehouse clerks—by walking toward danger instead of away from it, even when every rational instinct screamed warnings.

Especially when every rational instinct screamed warnings.

The game had found him, whether he was ready or not.

Time to discover if he was actually as good as he'd always believed.

PART TWO

THE NETWORK

Late Winter 2189
Outskirts of Beltmoire, CA

— ❖ —

The woman with one eye led Rhowan through the industrial district's back streets to a warehouse that looked abandoned from the outside but showed subtle signs of recent use: fresh tire tracks in the mud, windows boarded but not weathered, careful neglect that suggested purposeful concealment rather than genuine decay.

During the twenty-minute walk, Rhowan had tried several approaches to get her talking.

"So, what should I call you?"

Silence.

"I'm Rhowan, as you know. And you are...?"

More silence.

"Look, if we're going to work together..."

"We ain't working together." She cut him off without turning. "As far as I'm concerned, you're just cargo."

Cargo. Not a guest, not a recruit. Something to be transported and delivered. The distinction costs nothing to make and tells you exactly where you stand.

She moved like she'd mapped every sight line and escape route before they'd left the inn. Her clouded left eye tracked their surroundings. He could see it moving, catching pale shapes and shadows even through the milky damage. Her good eye focused ahead with predatory intensity that never wavered.

"Inside." She produced a key from her coat. "Keep quiet. Don't touch anything. Sit where you're told."

The interior redefined Rhowan's understanding of the situation. Tables arranged for meetings. Communication equipment more sophisticated than anything he'd seen in civilian use. Maps covering one wall with pins and markings that suggested operational planning on a territorial scale.

This isn't a crew. This is infrastructure.

A woman rose from behind one of the tables, and recognition hit Rhowan like ice water.

Tall, with dark auburn hair pulled back severely and sharp green eyes that missed nothing. Practical but well-tailored clothing. Composed authority that didn't need announcing.

"Thank you, Snips," she said.

Snips. So that's her name. It fits.

"Snips?" Rhowan turned toward his escort with renewed interest. "I don't suppose you'd care to share the origin story?"

Snips stared at him. Her good eye held his with the flat patience of someone deciding whether an insect was worth the effort of killing.

"Cute," she said finally.

"She'll gut you where you stand," the woman said with mild amusement that somehow made the threat more credible. "You're lucky she's in a good mood."

"Good mood? How can you tell?"

"She hasn't killed you yet."

Value assessment: these two have worked together long enough to share shorthand. The humor is real but so is the hierarchy. The woman gives orders. Snips executes them. And both of them already know more about me than I'm comfortable with.

"I'm Vanessa Kaine. Please, sit down."

The Vanessa Kaine. The one whose name had been circulating in political intelligence circles for months.

"Minister Kaine," he said, settling into the indicated chair. "This is considerably more distinguished company than I expected when I started investigating fish waste."

"Not yet. And if this conversation goes poorly, possibly never."

She opened a folder and spread documents across the table. "You've been asking questions about Canton Cusk processing waste. Your curiosity has been thorough. Also dangerously amateur."

"If I'd known it would lead to such distinguished company, I'd have been dangerously amateur much sooner."

Snips snorted. The first sound she'd made that suggested actual amusement.

Before Nessa could respond, the warehouse door opened. An exasperated voice carried across the space.

"Do you know how difficult it is to find a decent coffee shop in this town?"

A woman in her early thirties entered with a paper bag and coffee carrier, dark hair pulled back in a professional style. Everything about her bearing screamed senior government administration.

"Oh, have we started?" She glanced at her timepiece. "It's only 11:17, I thought we had until..."

She paused, staring at the timepiece face with a frown.

"Well, that's... odd."

"Victoria Colwell," Nessa said with a slight sigh. "Mr. Cade, Victoria handles our political coordination. Victoria, this is Rhowan Cade, information broker by trade."

"Regional information specialist," Rhowan corrected automatically.

"Pleasure to meet you, Mr. Cade," Victoria said, extending a hand. "Your investigation was quite thorough."

"Victoria, would you mind pulling Mr. Cade's file?"

"File?" Rhowan's composure wavered.

Victoria produced a folder from her bag with her other hand.

She brought my file in a coffee run. These people don't waste trips.

"Rhowan Cade, age twenty-two, resident of North York," Victoria read. "Employed as dockworker and warehouse clerk. Also operates as information broker specializing in shipping schedules, cargo manifests, and passenger movements across northern territories."

"That seems about right."

"Known associates include smugglers, customs officials, territorial contractors, and at least three members of the Andori mob. Recent activities include facilitating unauthorized cargo transfers, customs documentation irregularities, and what appears to be blackmail involving a territorial administrator's gambling debts."

Every word accurate. Every word leverage. These people haven't just been tracking me. They've been assembling me.

"I prefer to think of it as providing leverage for mutually beneficial arrangements."

"Your network extends throughout Hammison territory," Victoria continued. "Including connections to Governor Aldrich's infrastructure development contracts."

Nessa's expression shifted to genuine interest. "The Hammison connections. How deep?"

"Deep enough to understand how territorial politics actually work."

"Good." Nessa leaned back. "Because I'm running for the Ministry of Internal Affairs, and we need Governor Aldrich's endorsement. Two governors confirmed. The third is being blocked. Someone's applying pressure to Aldrich, and we need to understand what kind."

"And you want me to find out," Rhowan said. Not a question.

"Can you?"

"A few days for preliminary intelligence. A week to develop an approach that changes his mind." His confidence was building. "I have contacts in Hammison who understand the local political landscape. Connections you can't get through official channels."

Nessa smiled for the first time since he'd met her. An expression that transformed her face from professional assessment to something approaching warmth.

"Mr. Cade, I think you're going to fit into this operation quite well."

"One thing." Rhowan held her gaze. "If I deliver Aldrich's endorsement, what exactly am I helping to build?"

"A network capable of providing oversight where none currently exists," Nessa said carefully. "People who understand that certain territorial policies represent a threat, working together to implement countermeasures."

"That's deliberately vague."

"Yes it is. When do you leave for Hammison?"

✧

The train journey to CAD Hamilton took most of the day. Nessa spent portions of the trip reviewing documents she didn't share.

"You keep speaking in generalities," Rhowan said finally. "If I'm risking my regional independence for this, I need to understand what we're opposing. Not just what we're trying to build."

Nessa looked up from her documents. Studied his face.

"People disappear, Mr. Cade," she said quietly. "Regional brokers who ask too many questions about the wrong materials. Territorial administrators who won't cooperate."

She paused. Something in her expression that looked like personal knowledge.

"Enhanced individuals who pose problems for systematic operations."

"Enhanced individuals?"

"People with capabilities that certain parties find strategically useful. The materials you've been tracking are connected to programs that affect such people in ways that should concern anyone who believes in personal autonomy."

"And these programs operate without oversight?"

"They operate with oversight that ensures they continue operating. Which is why we need people in positions where they can provide different oversight."

By evening, they were in CAD Hamilton. Rhowan had never seen anything like it. Buildings that rose dozens of stories. Transportation systems that moved thousands of people efficiently. Organized prosperity that demonstrated what effective governance could accomplish.

The scale of everything here makes my territorial networks look like a kid's lemonade stand. But the principles are the same. Information flows. Leverage points. People who need things they can't get through official channels. The currency is just denominated differently.

Nessa led him through government districts to a residential area where officials and senior administrators lived. Victoria was reviewing documents spread across a dining table that had been converted into a campaign war room. Maps, voting tallies, biographical summaries covering every surface.

"Mr. Cade. I trust the journey was informative?"

"Increasingly so."

As the evening progressed, Rhowan found himself drawn into discussions of political strategy and coalition building. The stakes were higher than anything he'd imagined, but the principles were familiar.

Throughout the conversation, he remained aware of Snips in his peripheral vision. She didn't participate in the strategic discussions. She watched the windows.

Victoria's strategy session was winding down when Snips moved from her position near the glass. For the first time since he'd met her, she spoke without being directly addressed.

"They take children," she said quietly. "Families. Anyone who's useful to them. Process them into weapons. Tools. Things that ain't people anymore."

The silence that followed was absolute.

Snips turned from the window, her good eye fixing on Rhowan with an intensity that had nothing to do with threat assessment.

"That's what your fish waste and salt rocks make possible. That's what we're trying to stop. That's why people like you disappear when you ask too many questions."

Nobody moved.

Rhowan looked at Snips. At the damaged eye that someone had destroyed with deliberate precision. At the way she held herself, the stillness that wasn't calm but containment. At the personal knowledge that lived in every word she'd just spoken.

She's not describing something she investigated. She's describing something she survived.

"Governor Aldrich's endorsement," he said. "That's the key?"

"One key," Victoria said quietly. "There are others. But without institutional authority, we can't challenge these operations."

Rhowan sat with it. The warehouse. The maps. The communication equipment. Three women who'd built infrastructure for a war most people didn't know existed, fighting an enemy that turned human beings into strategic assets.

And they needed a twenty-two-year-old information broker from North York to help them get a governor's signature.

"When do I leave for Hammison?" he asked.

.

PART THREE

EYES OF BLUE

Early Spring, 2189

Hammison, CA

—— ❖ ——

Rhowan had always appreciated markets that operated in the gray spaces between official oversight and outright illegality. The Lower Loops of Hammison were exactly that: a sprawling bazaar built into the abandoned highway interchanges that had once connected the city's transportation networks before the Continental Authority rebuilt them using more efficient routes.

The concrete ramps and overpasses now served as multilevel markets where vendors sold everything from legitimate surplus goods to items that required no questions asked. Diesel fumes mixed with the scent of fried food and machine oil. The unique atmosphere of a place where survival trumped regulation.

Perfect for conducting business that required discretion.

Rhowan made his way through the warren of stalls to find Charles Anderson III: a mid-level political operative who claimed connections to Governor Aldrich's inner circle and who charged appropriate fees for facilitating introductions to people who mattered.

He found Anderson holding court at a cafe built into one of the old highway abutments, surrounded by minor political figures who made their living by being useful to more important people. Anderson himself was well-dressed beyond his circumstances, practiced charm concealing calculated self-interest.

Expensive suit, cheap coffee. The ratio tells you everything about his margins.

"Mr. Cade." Anderson rose with theatrical courtesy. "I received your message about seeking an introduction to Governor Aldrich. Please, join me."

Rhowan settled into the indicated chair, noting the way Anderson's companions melted away to provide privacy. Anderson actually did have the connections he claimed.

"I appreciate you making time. As I mentioned, I represent parties interested in discussing policy coordination with the Governor."

"Policy coordination," Anderson repeated, his tone suggesting familiarity with euphemisms. "And these parties would be?"

"People who understand that effective territorial governance requires cooperation between regions with shared interests." Rhowan gestured vaguely, allowing Anderson to assume whatever level of importance seemed appropriate.

Anderson leaned back, clearly preparing to deliver a speech he'd given many times before. "Well, Mr. Cade, I appreciate your confidence in my connections to Governor Aldrich's administration, but I think you may overestimate the ease with which such introductions can be arranged. The Governor is an extremely busy man..."

Rhowan's attention drifted as Anderson continued his explanation of bureaucratic obstacles.

"...which is why any approach to the Governor would need to be carefully coordinated through proper channels, with appropriate documentation..."

He's running out the clock to justify his fee. Standard gatekeeping. Let him talk while I calculate how much this introduction is actually going to cost versus what I can—

A flash of copper caught his eye.

A young woman moving through the market with a stride that made her stand out even in the chaos of the Lower Loops. Her hair was pulled back in a ponytail that caught the filtered sunlight like spun metal, and she moved with controlled grace that suggested someone comfortable in environments where situational awareness mattered.

Rhowan's mind went blank. Completely, thoroughly, uselessly blank.

"Hold that thought," he said, his voice coming out more breathless than intended. "I'll be right back."

He left Anderson mid-sentence and made his way through the market stalls, drawn toward the copper-haired woman with an inevitability that his professional training found deeply embarrassing. She was examining merchandise at a vendor's stall, accompanied by a tall, dark-haired man whose bearing suggested either military experience or a life that required similar levels of alertness.

"Excuse me," he said, deploying what he hoped was his most disarming smile. "I don't mean to interrupt, but I have the strangest feeling our paths have crossed before."

She studied him with ice-blue eyes that cataloged threats the way he cataloged value. Younger than he'd initially thought, but carrying experience beyond her years.

"Have they?" Amusement underneath wariness.

"Rhowan Cade," he said, extending a hand.

"Peri Blackwood." Her grip was firm. Calluses that spoke to hands-on work. "And I'm afraid you must have me confused with someone else."

"Well then, Red," Rhowan said, "perhaps we can start fresh."

"That's not my name," she said. Sharp edge.

"Your eyes," he said. The words came out before he could stop them. Not the practiced line. Something else. "They're quite striking."

For a moment, something shifted in her expression. A flush crept up her neck, dusting freckled cheeks with color. Then the walls slammed back into place.

"Do you practice that in mirrors?"

"That wasn't a line," Rhowan said, surprised by his own honesty. "That was just... true."

The tall man accompanying her shifted slightly, and Rhowan became aware he was being assessed with attention usually reserved for potential threats.

"And you are?" Rhowan asked.

"Kataero," the man replied, his voice carrying the gravitas of someone who didn't waste words. "Kataero Ota."

The name hit like a physical blow. His practiced smile froze.

"Kataero Ota," he repeated slowly. "You wouldn't happen to be... the Black Marshal?"

Kataero simply stood a little taller and stared.

Every story I've ever heard about this man is standing three feet away from me. And I've just spent the last two minutes flirting with someone under his protection.

"Well," Rhowan managed, his voice slightly strangled, "I'm sure most of what I've heard are just... colorful exaggerations." He attempted a laugh that didn't quite work. "You don't look nearly as terrifying as the stories suggest."

That was a lie. He looked exactly as terrifying as the stories suggested.

"We're conducting business," Peri said, her tone suggesting the nature of that business wasn't open for discussion.

"As am I." Rhowan was finding his footing again, the broker's instinct reasserting itself over the part of his brain that was still staring at copper hair and blue eyes. "Though I have a feeling that your business and mine might have more in common than any of us initially realized."

Kataero's attention sharpened. Rhowan realized he'd said something that carried implications he hadn't intended.

"Perhaps," Peri said carefully. "Though I find that coincidences in places like this are often less coincidental than they appear."

"I should return to my own business before my associate decides I've abandoned him entirely." Rhowan stepped back with a slight bow. "Until then, Red."

"Still not my name," Peri said, though her irritation was tempered by reluctant amusement.

✧

"I apologize for the interruption," Rhowan said, cutting off Anderson's continued explanation with renewed confidence. "Though I have to say, your concerns about approaching Governor Aldrich may be more pressing than either of us initially realized."

"How so?" Anderson asked, clearly annoyed but unable to hide curiosity.

"See that tall, dark-haired man over there?" Rhowan gestured casually toward where Kataero stood with Peri. "He's been watching our conversation with interest that suggests professional concern about political coordination in Hammison territory."

Anderson glanced in the indicated direction. Genuine nervousness replaced his previous confidence.

There it is. Anderson knows Kataero's reputation. Or at least knows enough to be afraid of men who stand like that.

"Who is he?" Anderson whispered.

"Someone who takes a very personal interest in political arrangements that affect regional stability. Interest that becomes uncomfortable for people who obstruct cooperation between parties with shared concerns."

"Are you threatening me?"

"Not at all." Rhowan's smile remained perfectly charming. "I'm simply suggesting that the bureaucratic obstacles you've been describing may be less significant than the practical considerations involved in facilitating productive cooperation." He leaned forward slightly. "So perhaps we could skip the extensive explanations and focus on how quickly you can arrange an audience with Governor Aldrich."

Anderson glanced again toward Kataero, whose presence seemed to loom larger now.

"I might be able to expedite the usual procedures," Anderson said carefully. "Given the apparent urgency of your business."

"Excellent. I'm confident that Governor Aldrich will find our discussion both informative and mutually beneficial."

Kataero Ota doesn't know he just expedited a political introduction. Peri Blackwood doesn't know she just became the most distracting thing in Hammison. And Charles Anderson III doesn't know that the man he's afraid of has absolutely nothing to do with my business.

Leverage doesn't need to be real. It just needs to be believed.

Anderson's already making calls. Meeting with Aldrich within the week. Three days ago I was a warehouse clerk. Today I'm brokering continental politics using a borrowed reputation and a woman I just met.

The principles are the same at every scale. Find the pressure point. Apply minimal force. Let other people's imaginations do the heavy lifting.

PART FOUR

THE ENDORSEMENT

Early Spring, 2189
Hammison, CA

— ❖ —

Governor Aldrich was competent, practical, and possessed of political instincts that had kept him in office through three election cycles. His office reflected the same qualities: well-appointed but not ostentatious, decorated with regional artifacts that demonstrated local pride without suggesting extravagance.

But there was something in the Governor's bearing that suggested this wasn't going to be straightforward.

Wariness. He's been expecting this conversation, but not looking forward to it.

"Mr. Cade." The Governor rose with practiced courtesy. "Charles Anderson tells me you represent parties interested in policy coordination. Please, have a seat."

"Governor Aldrich. I appreciate you making time." Rhowan settled into the indicated chair. "The parties I represent understand that effective territorial governance requires cooperation between regions with shared interests."

"Shared interests." The Governor's tone suggested familiarity with political euphemisms. "And what specific interests might those be?"

Appeal to his practical nature. Show him the benefits without revealing too much about the larger scope.

"Regulatory coordination between territorial administrations. Specifically, policies that affect maritime commerce, industrial development, and resource extraction in the northern territories."

The Governor's attention sharpened. "Maritime commerce covers significant economic activity in Hammison territory."

Good. He's engaging with the economic argument.

"Precisely. Minister Nessa Kaine has developed policy frameworks that could significantly enhance maritime commerce efficiency while maintaining appropriate oversight."

"Nessa Kaine." Governor Aldrich said the name thoughtfully. "I'm familiar with her work. Competent administrator."

He knows her reputation. But there's hesitation where I expected agreement.

"Mr. Cade," the Governor said, settling back with the expression of someone about to deliver unwelcome news. "I appreciate your confidence in Minister Kaine's capabilities, but I'm afraid I've already committed to supporting another candidate."

Shit.

"May I ask which candidate?"

"Minister Korvyn's office has been very persuasive about supporting Minister Caldris. He has strong credentials and established relationships within the current administration." Carefully neutral. "Hammison values stability in our ministerial partnerships."

Korvyn. Actively working against Nessa. This isn't hesitation. This is coordination.

"Governor, I understand the value of established relationships. But I wonder if you've considered what Minister Caldris's approach to oversight might mean for Hammison's diverse business interests."

"I'm not sure I follow."

"Minister Caldris represents continuity with current oversight methods. Which could mean increased scrutiny of arrangements that have previously operated with flexibility." Rhowan watched the Governor's expression. "Minister Kaine, on the other hand, understands the difference between effective oversight and bureaucratic interference."

There. A flicker of concern. He's worried about something.

"What exactly are you suggesting, Mr. Cade?"

Time to take a calculated risk.

"I'm suggesting that new leadership sometimes brings new priorities for oversight activities. Priorities that might focus on ensuring regulatory compliance rather than investigating historical arrangements that have served regional interests well."

The Governor's expression didn't change, but Rhowan caught the slight tightening around his eyes.

He knows about the arrangements. And he's worried about what fresh oversight might uncover.

"You seem remarkably well-informed about regulatory oversight for someone in information coordination."

"Information is my business. And the information I've gathered suggests that Minister Kaine's approach to oversight would be considerably more practical than what Minister Caldris might implement."

"Practical how?"

"Minister Kaine understands that effective oversight protects legitimate business interests by focusing on actual problems rather than investigating successful arrangements simply because they're profitable."

Let him draw his own conclusions about what constitutes 'successful arrangements.'

The silence stretched. Governor Aldrich rose and moved to the window, staring out at the late afternoon sky while weighing considerations that extended beyond endorsement politics.

Rhowan waited. Pushing too hard now could destroy whatever progress he'd made.

He's calculating. Cost versus benefit. Fear versus opportunity.

"The problem, Mr. Cade, is that commitments have already been made. Minister Korvyn's support comes with certain expectations about regional cooperation on matters beyond this endorsement."

There it is. He's not just politically committed. He's financially committed.

"Expectations that could become problematic if Minister Caldris decides to review those arrangements?"

The Governor turned back, his expression shifting to concern. "What makes you think he would?"

"Because that's what ambitious ministers do. They look for opportunities to demonstrate their authority. And reviewing profitable arrangements that aren't currently under oversight provides exactly that opportunity."

Governor Aldrich returned to his desk and withdrew a communication device that looked more sophisticated than standard governmental equipment.

Encrypted communications. He's asking for permission to switch sides. Which means he doesn't make these decisions independently.

The conversation was brief and conducted in coded language. But Rhowan caught enough to understand the Governor was explaining a change in circumstances that required "reevaluation of commitments."

When the call ended, the Governor settled back with the expression of someone who'd just made a decision with far-reaching consequences.

"Mr. Cade, I believe we can discuss providing Minister Kaine with the endorsement she requires."

Success.

"Complications can be managed," Rhowan said. "I'm confident Minister Kaine will demonstrate exactly the oversight approach that justifies your support."

As he prepared to leave, his eyes swept the office one final time. Most of what he saw was standard territorial administration. But the secured communication device was still partially visible, along with a document that had been exposed during the call. The header read "Regional Investment Coordination."

Line items showing payments to Minister Korvyn. Investment schedules for northern maritime development. And a term that made his blood run cold: "Ferrosalt extraction from red mud deposits: priority acquisition for research applications."

The connection between Korvyn, the financial arrangements, and the material acquisition I've been tracking. All on one page. All connected.

Rhowan committed the details to memory while maintaining his conversational departure.

"Governor, I'm confident that supporting Minister Kaine's candidacy will prove to be an excellent decision."

But as he left the mansion, Rhowan understood that the endorsement might be the least important thing he'd acquired today.

✦

The train journey back to CAD Hamilton gave Rhowan time to process both the success of his mission and the implications of what he'd observed in the Governor's office. The landscape rolling past the windows seemed different now. Not just territorial boundaries but a network of hidden connections that shaped policy in ways most people never suspected.

He was beginning to understand the game. The real game. And for the first time since Canton Cusk, he felt like he was playing it rather than stumbling through it.

The compartment was nearly empty. Late afternoon run. A few workers heading home, a woman with a canvas bag sleeping against the window three rows up. Rhowan spread his notes across his lap and started drafting the report for Nessa. Aldrich secured. The financial connections documented. The Ferrosalt link confirmed.

The seat beside him depressed.

"That one's taken," Rhowan said without looking up. The automatic smile. The easy deflection.

"No it isn't."

The voice was flat. Heavy. The kind of voice that settled into a space and made the space smaller.

Rhowan looked up.

The man was early thirties. Dark hair. A face that had collected damage the way some people collected debts: methodically, over years, with compound interest. He wore heavy work gloves, scarred leather, the kind that had seen use beyond what manual labor would explain. His body was dense and wrong-shaped in ways that suggested old injuries healed by people who prioritized function over comfort. He carried a cane, which he leaned against the seat between them with the ease of a man who'd stopped being self-conscious about needing it. The cane itself was unusual: metal shaft with a blue-black tint that caught the compartment light, the kind of specific coloring that said custom work, not factory production.

He sat down. Not beside Rhowan. Against Rhowan. Close enough that his shoulder pressed the armrest and his proximity felt like a statement.

Then something happened.

Rhowan never saw the man's hand move. Never felt a blow. But a sensation hit his legs, sharp and total, like stepping into water so cold it bypasses pain and goes straight to absence. Both legs. Simultaneously. The muscles went slack. Not numb. Not tingling. Simply gone, as if someone had disconnected them with a switch he didn't know existed.

He tried to stand. His brain sent the instruction. Nothing answered.

"I know who you are," the man said.

Rhowan gripped the armrest. Tried again. His legs were there. He could see them. They simply weren't his anymore.

Something clattered on the floor between their seats. Small. Glass. Still faintly smoking, the surface blackened and cracked like a spent lightbulb that had burned out from the inside. The man pulled off his gloves. Folded them. Set them on his knee with the unhurried precision of someone who'd just completed a routine task.

Unknown. The way you file a word in a language you don't speak.

"Apparently," Rhowan managed, still gripping the armrest, "I don't seem to have the pleasure of knowing who you are."

The man's mouth arranged itself into something that qualified as a grin the way a knife qualifies as a utensil.

"You'll connect it someday."

"Lovely. I look forward to it. Assuming I live through this."

"That depends on the next ten minutes." The man checked his watch. Functional. Heavy. A timepiece that measured urgency, not appointments. "We have ten minutes before the next stop. Your legs will work in about twelve." He looked at Rhowan the way you look at something you're deciding whether to use or discard. "Start talking, or I make sure they don't work again."

The threat wasn't performed. It was stated. The way you state the weight of a load or the temperature of a room.

"Well," Rhowan said. "Since you asked so politely."

"Canton Cusk. Ferrosalt. The processing facilities. The shell companies. The supply chain." Each word landed with the weight of a man who knew exactly what these things were. "Everything that calculating mind of yours has put together. All of it."

Rhowan's assessment ran fast: what does this person want, what does it cost to give it, what do I get back. But the calculation kept failing. No vanity to leverage. No anxiety to exploit. No visible agenda to redirect. The man's face offered nothing except intensity and a patience that felt like a door about to close.

"I'm usually more comfortable with transactions. I give you something, you give me something."

"I'll give you something worth more than anything in those notes."

"I'm listening."

"The Canton Cusk waste gets processed into precursor compounds. Ferrosalt stabilizes them. Together they produce a catalytic medium that interacts with compatible biological material." The words came out with the blunt precision of someone who'd learned this through his body, not from a textbook. "The medium is called Thermecine. And the compatible biological material is people."

The compartment went cold. Not the temperature. Something inside Rhowan.

"That's what your shipping invoices lead to. Facilities that process human beings into raw material for a substance that turns other human beings into weapons. The fish waste you've been so clever about tracking is the first step in a chain that ends with children on tables."

"You know this how?"

"Because I've been inside the machine."

He said it the way you say something that lives in your bones.

Rhowan talked. Gave him the shipping routes. The shell companies. Two Harbors Industrial. The Millhaven address that led to a machine shop. The financial patterns connecting territorial contracts to processing operations. He talked because the legs threat was credible and because the information about children on tables had just recalibrated every calculation he'd been running since Canton Cusk.

The man listened without taking notes. His eyes stayed on Rhowan's face, reading something there, checking it against whatever assessment he'd already made.

The train was slowing. A platform materializing through the window. "Nessa Kaine."

The name changed the man's face. Not dramatically. A shadow that moved through his expression the way weather moves through a valley: arrived, passed, left the landscape slightly different. Something between anger and grief carried so long it had become geography rather than emotion.

"I know you work for her," he said. "I've known her quite some time."

He stood. The movement was efficient but wrong. A body negotiating with its own damage. He picked up the cane. Leaned into it for one step before finding his balance.

"She carries a lot of secrets, your new employer. More than you know. More than she'll ever tell you." He looked down at Rhowan, still seated, legs still absent. "You shouldn't trust her."

The train stopped. Doors opened. Cold air pushing into the compartment.

He walked toward the exit. The cane tapped the floor with each step, a steady rhythm that counterpointed his uneven gait.

At the door, he paused.

"Your legs. About two more minutes. Don't follow me."

Then he was gone.

Rhowan sat in his seat. The spent glass cartridge was still on the floor, its surface cracked and blackened. He picked it up carefully. Warm. Lighter than it looked. The glass had a faintly bluish tint under the char.

He pocketed it.

The feeling returned to his legs in stages. Feet first. Then calves. Then knees. By the time the platform had disappeared behind the train, he could stand.

He stood. Sat back down. Picked up his scattered notes.

Under Nessa Kaine's name in his mental ledger, alongside *resources, authority, strategic capability, network*, Rhowan added a new entry:

Cost.

Whatever she was offering, someone had already paid for it.

○

He gave Nessa the sanitized version that evening.

The Aldrich endorsement first, which landed well: Victoria nodded with satisfaction, Nessa's approval was measured but real. Then the financial documentation. The Ferrosalt connections confirmed through territorial records.

Professional. Comprehensive. The kind of report that demonstrated competence.

Then, as if it had just occurred to him:

"Something else happened on the train back."

Nessa looked up.

"A man sat down next to me. Knew my name. Knew about Canton Cusk. Knew about the Ferrosalt connections." Rhowan kept his delivery casual. A curious footnote rather than the encounter that had rearranged his understanding of everything. "Wouldn't give his name. Early thirties, looked like he'd been through some hard years. Oh, and he had a cane."

The room changed.

Nessa's hands stopped moving. The particular stillness of someone who has just heard something they weren't expecting, and whose first instinct is to control every visible response before deciding which ones to release. Her face went through a sequence of adjustments so fast Rhowan almost missed them: recognition, then something older, then the mask coming back down.

From the corner, Snips made a sound. Short. Nasal. A snort that she turned into a cough that she didn't bother making convincing.

"What kind of cane?" Nessa asked. Her voice was level. But the question itself was the tell: she wasn't asking about his name or his threats or his intelligence about their operations. She was asking about the cane.

"Metal. Blue-black tint. Custom work." Rhowan watched her the way he watched everyone: for the gap between what they showed and what they held. "Unusual craftsmanship."

Nessa picked up her pen. Set it down. Picked it up again. "What did he want?"

"Information. What I knew about the supply chain. Gave me some in return." Rhowan paused. "He also said I shouldn't trust you."

"Smart man," Snips said from the corner. Almost inaudible. Almost.

Nessa studied the documents in front of her as if they required renewed attention, but her eyes weren't tracking the text.

"Did he say anything else?"

"That he'd been inside the machine. That he'd known you quite some time." Rhowan let the words settle. "He seemed... not hostile. Toward me, at least. More like someone delivering a warning he wished he'd received himself."

Nessa was quiet for a long moment.

"If you see him again, don't engage. Report it."

"Is he dangerous?"

"To himself, mostly." Something in her voice Rhowan couldn't price. "But yes. To everyone around him, eventually."

She returned to the documents. Subject closed. But Rhowan had seen enough. The stillness. The cane question. The pen picked up and set down. Whatever the man on the train meant to Nessa Kaine, it wasn't filed under *operational concern*.

It was filed somewhere deeper. Somewhere the Architect didn't let people look.

✧

"Korvyn," Victoria said, after the Regal discussion had been shelved and the strategy documents reopened. "He isn't just financially invested in these operations. He's personally invested."

"How so?"

"His family." Nessa's voice had regained its professional register, but the stillness from the cane discussion lingered underneath. "His sister's family was targeted by the same programs. The Eldains."

The Eldains. The same name connected to territorial resistance operations in the northern territories.

"Minister Korvyn is Regal Eldain's uncle," Victoria said. "Kaena Eldain was his sister. The enhancement programs didn't just target random families. They targeted families with genetic markers that made them valuable."

"So his financial involvement in the operations..." Rhowan began.

"Is complicated by the fact that those same operations destroyed his sister's family," Nessa finished. "Family justice might outweigh financial considerations if approached correctly."

That's the leverage. Personal loyalty versus financial interest. The most dangerous kind of pressure point: asking someone to choose between survival and integrity.

Rhowan looked at Nessa. At the woman who'd just heard a cane described and had to put down her pen twice before she could continue functioning. At the Architect who carried secrets that the man on the train had paid for with his body.

The Eldain connection. The cane. The blue-black tint of custom metalwork.

Something itched in the back of his mind. A connection his brain was reaching for and couldn't quite close. The man on the train and Minister Korvyn's sister's family and a cane made of metal that caught the light wrong.

He filed it. Incomplete. The way you file a thread that hasn't finished unraveling.

PART FIVE

THE BIG LEAGUES

Early Spring

CAD Hamilton, CA

— ❖ —

"The Council meets this afternoon to discuss ministerial appointments," Nessa announced, reviewing documents that had arrived with the morning post. "I want you there to observe the preliminary discussions."

"Official proceedings?"

"Preliminary session. Where the real decisions get made before the formal votes. Where information matters more than speeches."

"Surely you aren't inviting him to a Council session looking like this?" Victoria interrupted, studying Rhowan's appearance with professional horror.

Rhowan glanced down at his regional attire. Practical clothing that had served him well for dock work and territorial negotiations, but which clearly didn't meet the standards expected in continental government buildings.

Different arena, different uniform.

Victoria gathered her coat. "Come on. We're going shopping."

She moved through the government district's commercial establishments with the same efficiency she applied to everything: selecting a jacket in government blue ("projects reliability without being presumptuous"), trousers that fit properly, shoes that didn't announce dock work. The psychology of presentation applied to fabric and cut.

By the time they returned, Rhowan's appearance had been transformed, and he understood the principle beneath the tailoring. Presentation wasn't just about looking appropriate. It was about psychological positioning. Making people comfortable enough to reveal information while maintaining enough authority to be taken seriously.

"Much better," Nessa said. "Now you look like someone who belongs in a Council session."

"Time for the big leagues," Rhowan said. And meant it.

✧

The Continental Council chambers were everything Rhowan had expected from the center of territorial governance: soaring architecture designed to overwhelm, seating arrangements that reinforced hierarchy, lighting calculated for specific psychological effects.

Impressive theater. But the real power is in the relationships between the people, not the buildings.

The preliminary session was less formal than official proceedings but no less significant. Council members moved through the chamber in small groups, conducting conversations that shaped policy before votes were ever taken. Rhowan positioned himself where he could observe without participating.

The principles were familiar. Identify what people want. Show them how cooperation serves their interests. Apply pressure where necessary. The scale and sophistication were different, but the mechanics were the same ones he'd used in North York and Hammison.

He'd note that once and stop noting it.

His attention kept returning to one figure who commanded attention through presence rather than performance.

Minister Korvyn stood apart from the political maneuvering, watching the proceedings with detached assessment that spoke to military training. He participated when approached, but didn't seek out conversations. Professional courtesy without enthusiasm.

Not playing the game. Analyzing it.

Other Council members approached Korvyn with something approaching deference. Not just political respect. Recognition of someone whose opinion carried weight beyond normal legislative influence. When Chief Minister Ashford approached a small group that included Korvyn, Rhowan watched the interaction with intense focus.

She deployed the same subtle influence techniques he'd observed her using throughout the session: careful questions, strategic suggestions, the gentle shaping of consensus.

Korvyn simply listened. Polite. Attentive. Giving nothing away.

When the interaction concluded, Ashford moved on with practiced grace. But Rhowan caught the slight tightening around her eyes.

The master politician meets someone she can't manipulate. And she knows it.

Rhowan studied Korvyn for the rest of the session. The military bearing. The systematic observation. The wall that charm couldn't scale and leverage couldn't breach.

Something about the way Korvyn held himself reminded Rhowan of someone else. The same density. The same immunity to performance. A man who'd seen enough to be unimpressed by everything that impressed everyone else.

The man on the train had carried that same wall. Different damage, same architecture.

He couldn't articulate the connection. Filed it alongside the blue-black cane and the Eldain family name. Threads that hadn't finished unraveling.

✧

"Well?" Nessa asked as they departed the government complex. "What did you observe?"

"Minister Korvyn operates according to different principles than everyone else in that room," Rhowan said. "Ashford builds influence through consensus and subtle manipulation. Korvyn commands respect through demonstrated competence and principled independence."

"Which makes him harder to influence," Victoria said.

"It makes him impossible to influence through normal approaches," Rhowan corrected. "But it also means he responds to something different. He's not interested in political theater or careful manipulation. He wants direct communication about real issues."

And he's carrying the Eldain family's destruction the way the man on the train carried his cane. As a weight that defines how he moves through every room.

"The question," Nessa said carefully, "is whether we can approach him in a way that acknowledges both his political position and his personal history."

"Not leverage," Nessa added, before Rhowan could respond. "Understanding. There's a difference between exploiting someone's pain and acknowledging it."

The correction landed. Rhowan heard it, and for the first time, felt the difference between the two in a way that wasn't just semantic.

"Then help me understand," he said. "If I'm going to approach him, I need to know what I'm walking into."

"You know what you're walking into," Victoria said quietly. "You learned it on the train."

She was right. Korvyn's sister's family. The enhancement programs. The blue-black steel. The man with the cane who'd been inside the machine. The Ferrosalt extraction that connected shipping invoices to children on tables.

Rhowan knew what he was walking into. The question was whether he could walk into it honestly enough for Korvyn to let him through the door.

PART SIX

WHEELING AND DEALING

Early Spring, 2189
CAD Hamilton, CA

— ❖ —

Victoria had transformed her dining room into a campaign war room. Maps, voting tallies, and biographical summaries covering every available surface. She moved between the documents with precision that showed she understood exactly how political mathematics worked.

But for the first time since Khowan had met her, Victoria's composure showed hairline cracks. Her movements were slightly too quick. Her reviews of documents just a bit too focused. The kind of control that costs more energy than the thing it's controlling.

"Forty-seven Council members," she said, pointing to the master voting chart. "We need thirty-one for enhanced consensus on ministerial appointments."

"Current position?" Nessa asked.

"Eighteen confirmed supporters, twelve leaning favorable, nine uncommitted, eight leaning opposition." The tightness around Victoria's eyes was visible now. "Which leaves us roughly four votes short of the threshold, assuming the leaners break favorably."

Four votes. After Aldrich, that felt manageable. But Victoria's face says otherwise.

"In normal circumstances, the leaners break at sixty percent," Victoria continued. "But these aren't normal circumstances. Chief Minister Ashford has resources we can't match: government contracts, regulatory approvals, infrastructure funding. She can offer immediate improvements to people's lives. We can offer eventual oversight."

"What about Minister Korvyn?" Rhowan asked, studying the chart where the Military Affairs minister was marked in neutral gray. "How many votes could his endorsement swing?"

"Eight to ten, potentially twelve if his endorsement is enthusiastic." Victoria's voice went flat. "But he's remained completely neutral despite approaches from both campaigns. No one knows what would convince him to break ranks."

"What are our options without him?"

Victoria spread three documents across the table. When she spoke, her voice carried a brittleness that had nothing to do with policy analysis.

"Coalition building. Focus on regional development, practical benefits. Risk: Ashford can make the same promises with more resources. Direct confrontation. Use our evidence to expose the research programs. Risk: Ashford discredits the evidence and retaliates before the vote. Institutional pride. Build support around constitutional principles and checks and balances. Risk: abstract ideals don't overcome concrete benefits."

She gathered the documents. Her hands were trembling.

"Which brings us to the variable that could determine the outcome." She pointed to Korvyn's name. "If we convince him to endorse, we win. If we can't..."

The professional mask slipped entirely.

"If we can't, then all we have left is hope that people will choose principles over practical benefits." Her voice carried eight years of government experience compressed into six words. "Hope is not a strategy."

The room went quiet.

She's been carrying this for weeks. The vote counting, the strategy, the knowledge of what failure means. Victoria Colwell, who manages grain shipments and infrastructure proposals and the enthusiastic incompetence that passes for frontier governance, is cracking under the weight of something she can't manage her way through.

"I should talk to him," Rhowan said.

Victoria's head came up. "Rhowan, no. Minister Korvyn is not someone you can charm or manipulate. He's ended careers for people who tried."

"I'm not planning to manipulate him."

"You say that, but your entire approach to politics is based on manipulation. Identifying what people want, showing them how cooperation serves their interests, applying pressure." Victoria's voice carried unusual urgency. "Korvyn sees through all of it. He'll read your approach before you finish your opening sentence."

"Which is exactly why a direct, honest approach might work," Rhowan said. "If he expects manipulation, honesty is the one thing he won't be prepared for."

Victoria stared at him. "You're proposing to walk into the office of the most dangerous political mind in the Continental Authority and try sincerity."

"I'm proposing to walk into the office of a man whose family was destroyed by the same programs we're trying to stop, and tell him the truth." Rhowan met her eyes. "Not the politically useful version. Not the strategically calibrated version. The truth."

The man on the train told me the truth. No leverage. No performance. Just a man who'd been inside the machine, telling me what it did to people. And it changed everything I thought I knew.

Maybe that's what Korvyn needs. Not another politician applying pressure. Just someone who understands what the programs actually cost, and says so.

"That could work," Nessa said thoughtfully. "Though it requires extremely careful execution to avoid seeming like sincerity disguised as manipulation."

"When?" Nessa asked.

"Tomorrow morning. Before the preliminary vote count." Rhowan felt the familiar spark of a complex negotiation taking shape, but underneath it, something else. Something that felt less like calculation and more like conviction. "If we wait until the formal session, we lose the opportunity."

Victoria studied him for a long moment. The trembling had stopped. Something in her expression shifted from despair to assessment.

"You understand that if you approach him incorrectly, you could destroy any possibility of securing his support."

"Yes."

"And you understand that Minister Korvyn has personal reasons to be suspicious of anyone who brings up his family's situation."

"Yes."

"And you're going anyway."

"Someone has to."

Victoria gathered her biographical briefing materials. The efficiency was back, but it sat differently now. She wasn't managing a crisis. She was preparing someone for a conversation she couldn't have herself, with someone whose pain she could analyze but not reach.

"His office is in the Ministry of Defense complex, northeast wing," she said. "He arrives at seven-thirty. Takes his coffee black. Doesn't tolerate small talk."

"Noted."

"And Rhowan?" Victoria looked at him over the top of her reading glasses. "Don't try to be clever. Just be honest. If he smells performance, you won't get a second chance."

Nessa was quiet through the exchange. Rhowan caught her watching him with an expression he couldn't read. Not the Architect calculating an asset's usefulness. Something else. Something that might have been recognition of a quality she'd stopped believing existed in the people she recruited.

"Get some sleep," Nessa said. "Tomorrow's going to be long."

Rhowan left the apartment and walked through Hamilton's government district. The evening light painted the marble buildings in amber that made them look warmer than they were. He thought about Korvyn's wall. About the man on the train. About Victoria's trembling hands and Nessa's quiet assessment.

Tomorrow he would walk into a room where his tools wouldn't work. Where charm was useless and leverage was dangerous and the only currency that might buy passage was a truth he was still learning how to carry.

The broker in me wants to price the approach. Calculate the angles. Identify the pressure points.

The part of me that sat on a train while a man with a cane told me about children on tables wants to walk in there and say what's true. Even if it costs everything.

Especially if it costs everything.

PART SEVEN

THE GAMBIT

Early Spring, 2189

CAD Hamilton, CA

— ❖ —

Minister Korvyn's office reflected the practical efficiency of someone who approached problems with military precision. Maps on one wall showing territorial boundaries and resource distribution. Administrative documents arranged with systematic organization. No personal items. No decoration. A space designed for decisions, not comfort.

The man himself was tall, composed, with graying hair and bearing that suggested decades of comfort with difficult decisions. But what Rhowan hadn't expected was the careful assessment in Korvyn's eyes: the look of someone who evaluated threats before they announced themselves.

"Mr. Cade." Korvyn gestured curtly for Rhowan to take a seat. His voice carried the authority of someone accustomed to being obeyed without question. "I understand you have information that might affect ministerial coordination. You have five minutes."

Five minutes. Victoria said don't try to be clever. Just be honest.

Rhowan deployed his prepared approach. The same techniques that had worked with Governor Aldrich.

"Minister Korvyn, I appreciate you making time. What I've discovered involves financial patterns that could significantly impact your decision-making regarding upcoming ministerial appointments."

"Financial patterns." Korvyn's tone suggested he'd heard this song before. And didn't care for the melody.

"Coordination between territorial and ministerial authority that operates outside normal oversight channels." Rhowan pulled out his documentation, spreading papers across Korvyn's desk with the same efficiency that had impressed Victoria and convinced Aldrich. "These patterns suggest institutional overreach that someone with your background would want to address through appropriate ministerial cooperation."

Korvyn glanced at the documents without touching them. His expression growing colder with each passing second.

"Mr. Cade." Deadly quiet. "Are you attempting to manipulate my vote through carefully presented intelligence?"

"I'm providing information that demonstrates why Minister Kaine's candidacy serves military interests better than the alternatives. Someone with your strategic thinking would appreciate the long-term implications of..."

"Stop." The word cut the air. "Just stop."

The rehearsed presentation collapsed. This wasn't Aldrich. This was someone who'd seen through him immediately, completely, and was now looking at him like something to scrape off a boot.

Victoria warned me. She was right.

"What if I told you," Rhowan said, abandoning everything he'd prepared, "that there are bigger things at play than politics? That Vanessa Kaine has a plan, flawed as she may be, to challenge operations that..."

"Bigger things?" Something in Korvyn's voice shifted. Not dismissal anymore. Something darker. Heavier. "You want to know about bigger things, Mr. Cade?"

He rose from his chair. Moved to the window. When he turned back, his expression had transformed entirely.

"Sit down. And listen carefully, because I'm only going to explain this once."

Rhowan sank into his chair.

"You walked in here thinking you understood continental politics. You think this is about competing policy visions and parliamentary maneuvering. You think Minister Kaine represents oversight and Chief Minister Ashford represents the status quo."

He leaned against his desk with the bearing of someone delivering a military briefing that would get them both killed.

"You don't understand what this government has become, Mr. Cade. Or how it happened. Or what it costs to operate outside the approved narrative."

Korvyn's eyes fixed on Rhowan with laser intensity. "Chief Minister Ashford systematically captured institutional authority through the most sophisticated infiltration operation I've witnessed in thirty years of military and political service."

He moved to his maps. "Do you know how many territorial governors have been replaced in the past eight years? Seventeen. Governors who suffered sudden health crises, family emergencies, or career-ending scandals that required immediate replacement with 'interim' appointments."

His finger traced territorial boundaries, marking a geographic pattern across the continent.

"Hammison: Governor Marsh stepped down after his son was arrested for trafficking. The evidence appeared days after Marsh questioned agricultural subsidy allocations. Beltmoire: Governor Kent suffered a convenient heart attack two weeks after blocking infrastructure contracts. His replacement was sworn in before the funeral arrangements were finalized."

He returned to his desk. Settled in with the weight of someone who'd been carrying this knowledge for years.

"But governors are just the visible layer. Judicial appointments. Regional administrators 'promoted' to positions where replacements could be hand-selected. Municipal authorities who discovered that federal funding required accepting 'advisory personnel' who ended up making all the actual decisions."

"The Council would notice," Rhowan managed. "Other ministers would object."

Korvyn's laugh was bitter. "Half the current ministers owe their positions to Ashford's recommendations. The other half understand that opposing her results in career-ending investigations that somehow always discover financial irregularities requiring immediate resignation."

He leaned forward. "Do you know what they call me behind closed doors? Controlled opposition. The token dissenting voice that proves the system still tolerates democratic debate. My objections get recorded, my concerns get noted, and my opposition gets used to demonstrate that institutional authority responds to legitimate criticism."

He withdrew a folder thick with documentation. Transcripts of his speeches alongside broadcast reports that transformed his warnings into endorsements of the authority he was criticizing.

"They don't eliminate opposition, Mr. Cade. They weaponize it. My dissent serves their narrative more effectively than my silence ever could."

"And if you actually organized effective resistance?"

"Then I would become another career-ending scandal. Another example of why institutional stability requires careful oversight of individual ambition." Korvyn's voice carried deadly calm. "They'd make me destroy myself. Give someone enough pressure points, family, career, personal secrets, financial obligations, and they'll cooperate enthusiastically rather than face the consequences of resistance."

The weight of systematic coercion settled over Rhowan like a physical force.

"That's what you don't understand about Minister Kaine's candidacy," Korvyn continued. "She thinks she can work within this system to reform it. She thinks institutional oversight can constrain institutional authority."

"And you think she's wrong?"

"I think she's dead." Flatly. "Not immediately, and not obviously. But effectively. She'll either be corrupted, compromised, or eliminated. And her failure will be used to justify even stronger institutional control over future reform efforts."

The silence that followed was absolute.

"Why are you telling me this?" Rhowan asked finally.

Korvyn studied him for a long moment.

"Because in thirty years of politics, you're the first person who walked into this office without an agenda," he said quietly. "Everyone else comes here with leverage, with deals, with carefully crafted presentations designed to manipulate my decision-making. You came here with genuine concern about institutional corruption and family justice."

"And that matters?"

"It matters because genuine conviction is so rare in this environment that I'd forgotten what it looked like." Korvyn's voice carried something Rhowan hadn't heard before: not hope exactly, but the memory of what hope used to feel like. "Most people who discover the truth about this system either join it or get crushed by it. You're the first person I've met who might be naive enough to think it can actually be opposed."

"Naive."

"The best kind. The kind that doesn't know enough to quit."

Rhowan stood, understanding that the conversation was over but that something fundamental had been communicated beyond the words.

"Thank you for your time, Minister."

"Good luck, Mr. Cade." Korvyn settled back into his chair and reached for his documents. Already moving on. Already done with this conversation, or appearing to be.

✧

Rhowan left the ministry complex. The afternoon sun hit him like something he'd never seen before. The streets looked the same. They weren't.

He climbed the stairs to Victoria's apartment carrying more weight than he'd carried walking in. Victoria read his expression before he said a word. Her face fell.

"He dismissed me," Rhowan said. "Completely. Said our agenda would fail and create more harm than good. Said Nessa was effectively dead the moment she won, if she won. Said the entire system was captured so thoroughly that opposition from within was meaningless."

Victoria closed her eyes. The trembling was back.

"That's it, then," she said quietly.

"That's it."

The vote would happen tomorrow. Korvyn had made it clear: they would lose. The mathematics were wrong, the opposition was organized, and success would trigger responses that would destroy everyone involved.

Rhowan sat in Victoria's apartment and tried to calculate what had happened in that office. The broker's assessment ran the way it always ran: what was exchanged, what it cost, what he got back.

But the calculation kept failing. The way it had failed on the train when the man with the cane told him about children on tables. The way it failed whenever he encountered something that didn't fit the categories his experience had built.

Korvyn had told him everything. The scope of the capture. The controlled opposition. The systematic removal of anyone who resisted. He'd laid out the entire architecture of institutional corruption with the precision of a military briefing.

And then he'd said "Good luck" and gone back to his paperwork.

Was that a man explaining why resistance was futile? Or a man explaining exactly what needed to be resisted?

Rhowan couldn't tell. And not being able to tell was worse than knowing either way.

NESSA CODA

NETWORK COMPLETE

Late Spring, 2189 | Ministry of Internal Affairs
CAD Hamilton, CA

The formal swearing-in ceremony had been everything political theater demanded: soaring rhetoric about institutional independence, carefully orchestrated media coverage, and dignified pageantry that reminded everyone of the importance of constitutional governance. Three days after the Council vote, I'd taken the oath that made my authority official.

But the real ceremony happened in the smaller moments afterward. Victoria coordinating oversight schedules with precision, someone who finally had legitimate authority to back her capabilities. Rhowan establishing communication protocols with that peculiar ability of his to make connections form where none had existed before: regional networks suddenly aligning with continental objectives in ways that shouldn't have been possible but were.

The vote had been closer than we'd anticipated. Twenty-nine confirmed, with two abstentions that sent ripples of confusion through the chamber. But Minister Korvyn's endorsement, delivered with military precision just hours before the session, had swayed exactly the uncommitted members we'd needed.

Korvyn's statement had been brief. Professional. Focused on "constitutional oversight requirements" and "military interests in appropriate checks and balances." Nothing about family justice or personal history. But everyone in that chamber understood that when Korvyn spoke about institutional integrity, he spoke from experience with what happened when it was compromised.

Rhowan had returned from his meeting with Korvyn looking like he'd been through a war. Defeated, humiliated, convinced he'd destroyed everything we'd worked for. When the endorsement came through official channels the next morning, his shock had been almost comical.

"I don't understand," he'd said, staring at the formal statement with an expression that suggested his entire understanding of cause and effect had been upended. "He dismissed me completely. Said our agenda would fail and create more harm than good."

"Sometimes," Victoria had replied with something approaching maternal pride, "the most important conversations happen after you think they're over."

What she didn't say, what I suspected but couldn't prove, was that Korvyn had been testing Rhowan. Looking for something beyond political manipulation. Searching for evidence that someone could still approach him with genuine conviction rather than calculated self-interest.

In thirty years of continental politics, apparently that had become rare enough to be worth rewarding.

☼

Now, in the evening quiet of my new office, I could finally process what we'd actually accomplished. The Ministry of Internal Affairs: institutional authority that could challenge systematic operations proceeding without oversight for years. The Canton Cusk waste that had started Rhowan's journey now fell under my jurisdiction, along with the financial networks and policy coordination that made such operations possible.

The irony wasn't lost on me. To fight institutional coordination, we were building institutional coordination. To challenge people who operated through shadows, we were creating our own shadow operations. Every method we opposed, we were learning to deploy.

The question was whether we could do it without becoming another version of what we were fighting. I didn't have an answer. I suspected I wouldn't like the one I eventually found.

Victoria appeared in my doorway.

"The preliminary oversight schedule," she said, entering with efficiency that had become familiar. "Systematic operation review, financial pattern analysis, policy coordination investigations. Everything we need to begin comprehensive examination."

Everything we need to begin the war.

"Timeline?"

"Six months for basic framework, eighteen months for complete institutional review. Assuming cooperation from territorial administrations and minimal interference from Chief Minister Ashford's office."

"Cooperation we might not receive, and interference we can definitely expect." I reviewed her outline. "She won't let this proceed without response."

"Which is why the network matters as much as the authority. Official oversight backed by unofficial capabilities."

Creative resources. Another euphemism for operations that exist in the gray spaces between legal and necessary.

"There's something else," Victoria said, her tone shifting to the careful neutrality she used for sensitive intelligence. "Preliminary reports suggest Ashford is already coordinating response to your appointment. Operations being repositioned. Financial networks restructured. Coordination patterns modified to avoid ministerial oversight."

"How long before those modifications become permanent?"

"Twelve to eighteen months."

Eighteen months. A timeline that felt both impossibly short and endlessly long.

"And one more thing." Victoria consulted a page near the back of her folio. "Rhowan's field contacts flagged an incident in the eastern territories last week. A processing facility was hit. No casualties. Inventory destroyed. Equipment disabled."

She looked up from her notes. "The facility was connected to the Ferrosalt extraction network."

Something tightened in my chest. "Who?"

"No identification. The local report describes a single operative. Male. Moved with what they called 'unusual physical capability despite apparent mobility limitations.'" Victoria paused. "He left a message on the wall. Painted in something the investigators couldn't identify. Blue-black residue."

She didn't need to say the name. I could see it in her face, in the way she was watching me for a reaction she could measure.

I gave her nothing. Sixteen years of practice at giving nothing when his name came up.

"Anything else?"

"The message was one word." Victoria's voice was neutral. Professional. "'Remember.'"

I sat with that for a long moment.

Regal. Operating in parallel. Hitting the same war from his own direction, with his own methods, on his own terms. The weapon I'd built and lost and never quite stopped tracking. Out there somewhere with a cane made of blue-black steel and a grievance that would outlast both of us.

"File it," I said. "Monitor. Don't engage."

Victoria nodded and moved on to the next item.

After she departed, I remained at my office window. The government district settling into evening quiet. Somewhere in this maze of institutional authority, Shori was planning her response. Calculating. Preparing countermeasures.

And somewhere in the eastern territories, a man with a cane was burning processing facilities and painting one-word messages on walls.

The network was forming. Not just mine. Not just Shori's. Something larger. Multiple operations converging on the same targets from different directions, different methods, different motivations. Victoria's institutional precision. Rhowan's intelligence networks. Snips' operational capabilities. Korvyn's principled resistance.

And Regal. Always Regal. The one piece I couldn't control and couldn't predict and couldn't stop caring about no matter how many years of operational distance I put between us.

The title carried weight that extended far beyond political appointment. Minister of Internal Affairs. Two years ago I'd been planning operations from warehouse safe houses. Now I had an office with a view and the legal authority to do what I'd been doing illegally for a decade.

I should have felt triumphant. Instead I felt the particular heaviness of a woman who'd just been handed the tools to build something she wasn't sure she had the right to build.

Outside, Hamilton settled into evening. Inside, the work continued.

It always did.

ABOUT THE AUTHOR

JT Baldwin spent thirty years carrying the world of Blood & Steel before he ever wrote it down. The first sketches lived in notebooks shared with his twin brother — game designs, comic characters, half-built mythologies that never quite let him go. They matured in silence through a career that took him from military service to long-haul trucking across the country, the kind of work that leaves a person alone with their thoughts for ten hours at a time. The characters traveled with him.

The Blood & Steel saga foundation is built on three interlocking series: the Ironforged novels, beginning with *Wilted Crowns*; *The Palisade Journals*, a five-novella collection charting the decades of conspiracy and resistance that shape everything to come; and *Forged in Blood & Steel*, an ongoing collection of short stories from the world. He believes the best stories leave readers with something worth thinking about long after the last page — and that the second read should be richer than the first.

He lives in southeastern Minnesota with his wife, where the world keeps growing and the winters are too damn cold and long.

www.ingramcontent.com/pod-product-compliance
Lightning Source LLC
Chambersburg PA
CBHW022045170626
46808CB00003B/1367